First published 1994 by Walker Books Ltd
87 Vauxhall Walk, London SE11 5HJ

This edition published 2009

2 4 6 8 10 9 7 5 3 1

Illustrations © 1989 Maureen Roffey

Text © 1994 Walker Books

The right of Maureen Roffey to be identified as illustrator of this work
has been asserted by her in accordance with the
Copyright, Designs and Patents Act 1988.

This book has been typeset in Avant Garde Gothic

Printed in China

British Library Cataloguing in Publication Data:
a catalogue record for this book is available from the British Library.

ISBN 978-0-7445-3587-7

www.walker.co.uk

Busy Babies

Maureen Roffey

WALKER BOOKS
AND SUBSIDIARIES

LONDON · BOSTON · SYDNEY · AUCKLAND

 Two busy babies

learning to draw;

 a brush for a teddy,

a brush for the floor.

Two little babies

playing with their clothes;

 sand in the sandpit,

sand in their toes.

 Two noisy babies

playing with pans;

 cleaning teeth

 and washing hands.

 Two happy babies

 playing hide-and-seek;

 tired little babies

fast asleep!